ESCAPISM
By Daniel Stocks,
Aliyah White, and
Rowan Costen

Contents:

Streetlights at Midnight

Daniel Stocks

Looking for someone else's love is like
endlessly walking through an empty street.
The empty streets which harbour the subtle
sympathies of strangers, the tragic feeling of
loneliness, and the knowledge of not being
good enough.

But learning to love yourself is the same
empty street, illuminated by stolen sunlight
and the warm glows of streetlamps. And now,
after realising my worth, I dance, barefoot,
down the middle of the road, headphones
blasting music; hands brushing through the
dancing headlights and streetlights; the subtle
embraces between the sunrise and the starlit
sky. Every step is a stride into complete
freedom, further and further into ecstasy.

The silence lets me feel the bass of the music, the cool air flying through my fingers. I feel everything, yet nothing at all. I see everything, hear everything, smell everything, taste everything, yet remain so blissfully unaware and ignorant to everything around me.

The mood changes as each song plays, my eyes never leaving the sky. I feel my heart reaching for the stars, my legs walking towards the orange horizon, my fear staying in the darkness behind. Streetlights begin to flicker off, cars begin to drive up and down the road, people begin to start living, breathing, walking mindlessly in every direction. It's me, and only me, walking in a sudden sea of people, watching as everyone walks into their prison, as I run and dance into the light, until I find my escapism

Breathing Colours

Daniel Stocks

Dull, empty, grey. The sky looks bleak
through my windowpanes. Clouds cover
the light. I haven't slept, seen daylight
twice, and now I'm getting ready to fly.

I get ready, put my skinny jeans on. Shoes
on, run out the door. I say goodbye as I
leave, knowing I won't come back until
the morning begins to glow.

I run to see them, taking in the summer
heat, the cool breeze, and the half of what
I need to see to get there.

We're together, until were not, they leave, come back, and then go off. I'm alone, the darkness surrounding me. I see eyes in every direction, feel voices in my head, feel the vibrations of the air. They're back, they're eyes full of life, watching as the stars pass us by.

Then one goes, heavily asleep, and now we wait until the sunlight decides to greet. I begin to fade, wanting sleep and wanting shade. But the beauty in the sunrise, in their smiles, watching as the colours of the sky embrace the emotions of our high.

I see them, smiles on their face, smoke covering their eyes. The laughter, the colours which pulse through the ground.

The sky is blue, the chilling cold the only thing I feel on my body. One more, and the colours come to life, dancing around the world. The ground breathes, the leaves embracing each gust of wind. I lean back to look up into the sky, feeling the warmth of the wind on my thighs. The laughter fades out as the sun burns orange. I still feel their presence, but we remain quiet, all under the same sky, but without the same minds.

Take another, and I stay in my seat, my veins pulsing, feeling their body heat. Their empty words are full of love and life, my empty heart still beating as it becomes night.

We walk down unfamiliar streets,
pretending we know where were going.
We can go back, but we keep at our feet,
only sitting down to take it all in, the
ridiculous, the heat.

I feel sick, I feel heavy. I feel putrid, feel
my body ready. They cry, they weep,
about their woes and their lack of sleep. I
nod along, waiting for the noise to stop,
waiting for the ground to stay still. Keep
the sick in, run away from the people. But
they won't shut up, and I can't leave them.

They won't stop trying, they need
someone else, why the hell will no one
pick up? 24 hours and I feel like I haven't
even blinked, let alone slept, let alone
been free.

They've gone, and once again I'm on my feet. I made them feel like a burden, I cry as I walk so when I get there I can sleep. They made me feel insignificant, they made me feel like I wasn't good enough, they made me feel guilty, they made me feel numb. I don't complain, I endure the heat, but when I say I need someone, they begin to bleat.

But it's my fault, and I take another swig, waiting for the colours to fade, waiting until I feel bleak. But the pavements don't stop moving, the world continues to breathe, the colours in the sky triggering every second of my heartbeat.

I'm on my own, staring at moving walls and creaking doors. One more and I'll feel nothing more. I hear voices outside, talking about last night, and I feel as if I was there, dancing underneath the streetlights.

I can't feel my skin, my heart won't stop beating, my eyes dart from side to side. My head is full of thoughts, philosophical but meaning nothing, but on my mind is the colours, the spinning lights, the patterns which make me realise that I'm not alright.

I feel sick, something moves underneath my skin. Water. Need water. I shove my face into the sink, losing my breath as I begin to scream. I hear everything, but nothing at all, all the screams in my head, but not the water pouring on the floor.

I can't look them in the eyes, I speak clearly so they think I'm fine. They know, they've seen it a million times. The only thing I can taste is cold and spice, can barely concentrate enough to put the spoon to my face. They ask if I'm fine, I say "I'm hungover" as if that's any more alright. They believe me, they haven't seen my eyes.

I run upstairs, throw everything up again. Hold my neck as I heave, my legs hurting more than my knees. Drawing blood just to feel myself breathe, my stomach churns, my emotions unclean.

I cry, I scream, I watch as they are fine. Watch as they laugh and dance, whilst I die. They don't care, they didn't even ask, whilst I'm on my own, on a bathroom floor, they're living their best life.

I watch shows that used to make me laugh, feel my breath begin to leave, feel my heart continue to pound. From every tear that falls, and every fake smile, no one knows I'm not alright.

It takes a simple text, just ask me if I'm alright. Do you really care if I live or die? I already know I won't get help, I'm losing my mind, watching them be happy whilst I die inside.

I disgust myself, I feel my brain crunch, every pump of blood through my veins is a shard of glass. My voice echoes through my brain, every slight noise triggers me, every single drop of rain.

Awake for 36 hours, I feel my chest begin to numb. My eyes are heavy, my breath steady, my heart acting like a shotgun. I can barely lift up my hands, can't fight back the tears, watching as everyone moves on, whilst I can't get to my feet.

48 hours awake, my eyes dry. I still feel my heart beating from my mistakes made last night. The smell of the empty bottles, the emotions I felt underneath the stars, are meaningless from all that I've lost, my pain obvious if someone just looked into my eyes. My breath begins to lighten, my heart begins to slow, I watch as the colours of my skin fade back into the unknown. The colours of the sky are now grey and bleak, the clouds cover the sun, I can feel my hands and feet.

They've been vibing, they've been having a good time. I've been left behind.

Now the colours have gone, now the world is just as dark, I see that the temporary escapism; the false emotions and the beating heart, made me feel emptier, made me feel cold. Now I hide underneath my blanket, watching the world turn; watching them move on.

Reckless

Daniel Stocks

It might be the rebellious attitude to life, it might be the recklessness, but there is something so raw about feeling completely at ease, feeling completely free. It's that childish attitude to life, the lack of commitments and responsibilities: the fact I can run through silent roads; dance in between trees, fly around lampposts, listen to music sitting underneath streetlights; watch my legs dangle over walls, far too much air between my feet and the ground; on top of parking lots, watching the world stay still.

There's something so pure about listening to music at 2am, with friends who you don't have to constantly try with, people you always have something to talk about, or even just sit in silence and be in each other's company. Sharing memories underneath the stars, saying "this is why I decided to stay".

There's something so sad about constantly missing the ones who hurt you. Why do we stay in situations which make us feel bad? Why do we continue to let the same people hurt us, over and over again? Who said we had to put up with it? In the end, what is really keeping us there? Is it history, what it used to be like, or the fact we don't know different?

There's something amazing, that the ones you love are always the first ones you go to for an issue. The first I call, the first I text, the first I voice note. There's something so unbelievably comforting about knowing that in any situation, in any state of mind, I have the people, and they know that the roles reverse, and it still works the same.

There's something beautiful about our world, despite the hate that riddles the constant need for power, despite the toxicity of holding power over others, even though people think that they're owed anything.

Our world, which is so full of life, full of amazing creatures, sights which if they were in a movie would be a work of fiction. Even laying underneath the stars, as the trees reach towards the sky, being right next to someone, is something that makes you think that life isn't real.

Sometimes all it takes is a positive attitude, a close bond, and a clear sky, to realise that the only escape you need is from yourself, from the four walls that keep you away from the outside, from the people that make you feel worthless. Nothing is permanent.

Every second counts.

Overthinking

Daniel Stocks

I can't get out of my own mind. Sitting between four walls, staring at the ceiling, just waiting for my head to shut up. If it's not me overthinking, overanalysing, overcomplicating situations, my mind creates situations, tortures me over possibilities, over scenarios which couldn't happen.

I hate my own mind, and I can't escape it. It isn't like a person you can just avoid; it isn't the stranger on the street that makes you cross the road. Its stuck, I'm nothing without my brain, and I hate it.

I can't stand myself, to the extent where I've realised why I'm unbearable to be around. I say the wrong things, and then beat myself up about it, I take on people's problems to avoid confronting my own. Sometimes I have to think, am I psychic, smart, or is one of the scenarios I pulled out of my head at 3am, purely because I have to make myself upset.

I say I can't stand being alone but lock myself up and hide away. I can't get out; I can barely even distract myself anymore. Everything is too much, its torturous. I wish it would just shut up, I wish I could escape, I wish it could just all go quiet, even for a second, just so I can think. Think about anything else. I need quiet to think, I need my head to just shut up, so I can think. I just want to sit and think. Please just shut me up, I'm sorry, I just want to escape.

Empty people

Daniel Stocks

Numb, feelings that don't matter. Nothing makes me happy, or at least happier. Just let go.

Drinking on an empty stomach, feeling your head spin outside of your body as you fall to the ground. Falling on people to fill empty spaces, pills to fill the silence.

I watch my blood pump through my veins, listen to my heartbeat when I'm alone; when its quiet. I remind myself that even when I'm at my worst, I'm alive. That's more than they can say at least.

But when you feel the laughter ripping through your walls, when you see their genuine smiles, when you can see their energy light up around you, their eyes brighten just a little. Even if there's so much black that you can't see the colour in their eyes, even if what they're thinking is so cold, their skin numb and their minds filled with synthetic emotions. You make a difference.

When you know that you're both running, you still found yourself, even if that's just running through empty streets, playing on empty swings, laughing with empty people.

Do you ever just look at your life and think "how did I get here?" Sometimes it would be a good thing: looking at the beauty of nature; experiencing something so incredible its almost indescribable; looking at the people around you and the love you get to have.

Other times, its staring at a blank wall, listening to the ticks of a clock, watching as the darkness slowly becomes light, because once again, your thoughts have kept you up, your brain picking apart every minute, your heart breaking at scenarios that haven't happened. There's just nothing else to do but think "why am I still here?"

Today. I knew, not only physically how I got here, but why. It's because of him, but also maybe them. They're the reason I'm surviving, the reason I'm tolerating it. Call it stubborn, call it pride.

Hurt, pain, tears, tiredness. Crying, laughing, screaming, silence. Emotions so complex they're simple, feelings justified but actions intolerable. Understanding how but not why. All the things you're alive to feel, even if it feels like you're just falling.

At least I'm not empty.

Rain in Summer

Daniel Stocks

It's getting late at midday. I can't love myself,
so how can I try to love you? How empty you
look when you smile at me. Pictures never
looked so grey.

I'm sorry I'm boring when I'm sober. I'm only
good enough when it's over. I'm colder when
I'm closer. Will you still love me when I'm
hungover?

Why when I'm with you, does it rain in
summer?

Midnight adventures and drunken trips. I'm
only myself around you. Full moon and you're
the only one I care about. When you leave my
arms, you seem so out of place

But then I'm boring when I'm sober. The calls
just don't last as longer. I'm only better when
it's over. Since when did my love become so
hungover?

Leave me in the winter, when I'm cold and
need you again. Hold me when it rains in
summer, when we can catch up to the sunrise,
look up and find our star signs.

Fugitive

Daniel Stocks

Part I: Hunted

Memories. I remember everything from that day, everything from the smell of cider, the speech on the television, the laughter of my friends as we sat in a circle laughing, playing drinking games. But we were so quiet, we were so paranoid. Every flash of light, every small noise that echoed through the silent streets. The noise of the helicopters which constantly hovered around the town. The constant sirens that plagued the peace. I jumped as every sense was overwhelmed with fear, paranoia. Scared of getting caught.

The paranoia started at the announcements from the Governments of the world. From then I memorised every detail and every noise. April 18th, 2020. April 18th. April 18th at exactly 4.58pm. They arrived at my door, I smiled and let them in. No one was noisy, no one drew attention. My friends came to my front door under the cover of darkness.

I remember the television saying, "police will enforce," and "police now have the power to arrest anyone suspected with the virus without warrant", and "people arrested will be used in a trial to find a cure". I remember the panic in Eloise's voice when she asked if we would be safe. I remember how sincerely I said.

"We will not get caught."

All these memories and only one stuck in my mind like a bad dream, one of those ones that just keep repeating and repeating. Like feeling suicidal and just imagining all these different scenarios you could die in. I couldn't escape the noise of her scream, in the pitch black. Why she went outside, I will never know. She just did. The sudden flashes of light from a helicopters spotlight, the smashing of glasses as we stumbled to try and hide. Hide from them, the people who once swore to protect us. They swore. They promised.

I hushed everyone, told them to be quiet. Told someone to help Kacy, help her with the inherent panic that comes along with not knowing what has just happened to your best friend. Quietly, yet swiftly, moving a bookshelf was a task, crawling into a small space underneath the house was another, pulling the bookshelf back towards the wall when inside the space underneath the house. That was borderline impossible.

We crawled into an empty space, enough space between the house floor and the concrete below for us to breathe. I started telling everyone to stay quiet while I would go to look what was happening through the cracks in the bricks.

Footsteps smashed against the stairs above us, dust falling from the ceiling and into my eyes. Kacy was almost in tears, around her huddled the others, comforting or quieting her. We had to be silent. We depended on the silent. Through the cracks I could just about make out the voices that were coming through the Police Radios.

"Oh fuck." Ella broke the silence with sincere panic.

"What?!" Chloe whispered in-between the gaps in Kacy's panicked breathing

"I left the fucking vodka on the stairs, and my lighter."

"Not really our biggest issue right now Ella." Eloise sighed, looking towards the ceiling at every bump.

"You mean, my vodka." I muttered under my breath, but that reminded me we needed supplies.

I started making a list in my head of what we would need, what we would want, and what we had to leave behind. I heard a grunt and some footsteps on the decking behind the wall. Kacy immediately stopped breathing.

A footstep then echoed into the empty space between us and the outside. I closed my eyes, wishing, hoping, needing them to not be able to see us.

No flashlight, no speech, no voice.

Nothing.

Sighs of relief swept through everyone's minds, but we needed supplies.

"There's no footsteps upstairs anymore, I think they're all in the garden, who's coming with me to get supplies?" I asked quietly.

"Fuck that, I'm not dying today." Megan almost shouted.

"Shut it Meg." Chloe hushed before jabbing her in the side.

"I'll come." Aliyah had been quiet this whole time, but she had a bravely-nervous look on her face. I thanked her, and we moved the bookshelf, wary of the flashlights hitting the windowpanes.

"What do we need?" She asked, grabbing my grey bag, and then my larger purple bag, from the top of the stairs. She immediately shoved the bottle of vodka into the bottom of the bag, smiling.

"I'll get food and water from the kitchen, you get clothes, blankets and the first aid kit from upstairs, and don't tell Ella about the vodka."

"Okay, I'll meet you in the hole in the wall in five."

"Ye…" my teeth sunk deep into my lips, the metallic tang filling my mouth, as I heard one dreaded noise.

The cacophonous sound of a gunshot, the metal clang as the bullet hit the ground, and the piercing scream of one of my close friends, reverberated throughout the ghostly night sky. I ran, ran for the cupboards and grabbed every canned food I could, every bottle of water, every inch of food I could manage. I grabbed kitchen knives, ran to the gun cupboard near my front door to grab hunting knives and two handguns. I heard Aliyah rummaging through the linen closet, grabbing soap, plasters, safety pins, everything we needed.

My back door opened; the noise of the lock opening ricocheted off of every wall.

Aliyah shuddered and hit the hanging light with the linen door, shattering it. The back door smashed shut, footsteps running up the stairs. Objects bounced off of the walls downstairs, I could see the lights of gunshots, piercing through the rooms. A wave of panic, or maybe adrenaline, and I was ready for blood.

"Hide, now." I whispered to Aliyah, before we crawled behind the wardrobe in my room.

It was claustrophobic, terrifying. I didn't know whether it was my heartbeat or Aliyah's which was pulsating. Mine, had to be. I held my hand out to Aliyah, a gesture to make sure she was okay.

She just looked straight ahead, squeezing
my hand, staring into the darkness.
Flashlights blinked through the glass,
shattered the darkness in the room, shone
from underneath the door. I heard more
gunshots, more radio noises.

And then I heard "all clear."

The footsteps died down, only one man
left patrolling the house because he had an
"inkling". He must've been new, no one
paid attention to his gut. I did. He came
into my bedroom, opening my drawers
and rummaging through my things.

I almost cried, but the invasion of my privacy wasn't going to get me caught. Aliyah grabbed a knife from my back pocket, put her hand over my mouth in a demonstration. I put my thumbs up, and saw her brown eyes glint red as we snuck through the darkness, knives in hand, ready to slash and rip apart what was making us question whether we would survive or not. He caught my eyes, tried to shout, but I grinned as I stabbed into his stomach, into his heart, into his neck.

"Oh shit, oh shit, oh shit, we need to run." Aliyah said, the blood on her hands dripping all over the carpet.

"We need to wash our hands first."

"Yeah probably." She said, snapping the neck of the man with a gun, making sure he could never even think about shooting us, or warning the others. We weren't exactly bloodthirsty, nor murderous. We were being hunted, and what's better than hunting the hunters.

Flickers of light from the hidey hole revealed the relieved smirks on my friends faces. I threw myself into the hole and yanked the bookshelf back into the wall. The relieved look quickly grew concerned. Grew fearful when they saw my blood-stained hands. Grew panicked when they heard the shouts of police officers, screaming nothing but "Man down!"

"What did you do?" Amanda questioned, an anger consuming her face. She was angry, scared, annoyed, confused. We all were.

"Killed him, he was going to kill us." Aliyah stammered as she put her hand on my shoulder.

"We had to; we have to survive." I was scared, I will admit, mostly about how much I enjoyed it. I saw the look in my eyes in the mirror as I stabbed into his body, saw Aliyah's snarl as we did everything we could. Simply to survive. All we needed was to survive.

"Survive?! What the fuck is happening, this is insane!?" Megan stuttered, her annoyance feeding into her fear.

"We can't stay here forever, we need to leave," Amanda said, pulling out her phone, "phones on aeroplane mode everyone?"

The flashes of phone screens lit up the room for just about a minute. Amanda was in brainstorm mode, and we were getting out of this mess. We had to. We just had to.

"They found the body, that means they're busy assessing the situation upstairs and searching the house." Amanda started explaining, writing it out in her notes app. "It's easy to remove the bricks there, and the hole in the wall is only covered by a protective cover, we can sneak out into the garden, but what then?" I added, to which Chloe kicked the wall down in one kick.

"I didn't mean do it now, but thanks."

"Dan, did you ever fix that gap in the fence behind the decking?" Ella asked, remembering when we climbed over it to sneak out at a sleepover to get drunk in the park.

"Me, fix things." I laughed.

"We escape through the hole in the wall, through the gap in the fence, there's a blind spot on this side of the house anyway so as long as no special forces are in the garden we're set." Amanda had her eyes on a way out, at a specific time.

"Aliyah, did you grab anything that can smash or be used as a distraction?" I asked, thinking tactically.

"Hell yeah of course I did." She said, unzipping the bag and pulling out three firecrackers and a smoke grenade my brother had kept from a paintball game a while back."

"This is about to get amazing." I almost screeched with glee, pulling my lighter out from the front pocket of my bag.

"Dan, this is the only time I'm trusting you with explosives." Amanda said, before laughing.

"And that is why it's a good thing to have a psychotic bitch on the team." Ella said, hugging me before her and Amanda scouted the garden to make sure we could make a getaway.

"All clear"

We quietly, but swiftly, got out from underneath the house and hid around the side, making sure no one was around, either in the apartments behind or the road ahead. No one.

"We ready for chaos?" I said, pulling the lighter towards a firecracker, before launching it up into the house. It landed on the ledge of a window. Everyone was about to sigh, or call me an idiot or something, before they saw the frankly psychotic grin. The windowpanes shattered into pieces, enough room for me to easily throw two more, and a smoke grenade.

"These damages are about to get expensive." I laughed, watching the curtains succumb to a violent blaze and smoke filling the house like a smoker's lungs.

"Now, Now!" Amanda said, grabbing my wrist and drabbing me, making me vault over the decking and into the undergrowth, where the others were hiding behind the wall.

"We made it off your property, now what?" Eloise chimed in, probably the first time since she commented on the alcoholism in the group. Not our faults to be honest.

"The woods, cover from air police, and we can hear ground police before they reach us?" Megan suggested.

"Megan, you don't know how much I love you right now, you're a freaking genius!"

"Remember when it snowed and we went sledding that time it snowed, we could sneak into the woods through that way when I fell into the ditch!" Megan and I then proceeded to laugh about how stupid my face was when I sledded down the hill.

"Yeah, let's do that." Amanda said, before Chloe stopped her from walking out into the roads.

"If were escaping, were doing it well, are there any security cameras that will catch us?"

"There's only cameras by the entrance to the apartments, but we can turn them off by turning the power off inside the utility cupboard outside."

"Dan, why do you know this?" She asked, before deciding she in fact did not care, and didn't want to know.

"I'll go turn them off."

I ran across the road, cautious of the entrances which could spot me.

Luckily it was dark, and I broke the lamp posts a while ago. That was the last time I was ever allowed to kick a ball. Not that I wanted too anyway.

Opening the cupboard, I was immediately met by cobwebs and dust, but there was a flashlight by the corner bins. I closed my eyes, wished myself luck, and walked into the complete darkness, shutting the door behind me. I grabbed the flashlight, hitting it a few times before the batteries kicked in. The switch was right in the corner, just behind a massive spider. I hate spiders, but I think I hate the idea of dying at the hands of the special government forces more. I flipped the switch, nothing. The spider touched my hand, and while I felt like screaming, I used my fear instead to kick the spider and break the circuit board. All the lights in the apartments flickered off, and then burst. I kicked the door down and signalled for the group that we had to go now before someone came to check what happened. Aliyah was the last to cross, and I will be honest we almost got caught by an old lady, but Chloe managed to sneak up behind her and push her into the mud, before running into the woods.

We all ran, ran as fast and as far as we ever had before. Ran so deep into the woods, the moonlight and stars faded into insignificant yet suffocating darkness. Fortunately for us all, I "forgot" to put the torch back. By the time we were all winded by the exercise, we were all walking, hands holding, together.

We made sure to be quiet, Kacy had calmed down, and was mostly just numbing herself from the trauma. I could feel the tension in Amanda's hands, and the nerves which shook through Ella's whole body. I felt absolutely fine, I felt sick feeling that I was almost enjoying it.

Although, I had always wanted a reason to escape it all, and now I was. And I felt powerful. Aliyah came up to me and whispered that she knew how to get to a motorway service-station on the other side of the woods.

"Hey, Aliyah's got a point, we could do hitchhike in a lorry!" Eloise had a bright look on her face, almost optimistic.
"Or we could, you know, sneak in so no one knows we are in there, so we don't get caught or snitched on?"
"That's illegal!" Eloise sighed.

"Eloise, I'm sorry to break this to you but I've just murdered someone and burnt down my house, Chloe assaulted an elderly woman, and we are literally runaways from the government, Legality is the last thing on my mind right now. God, I need a drink."

"Chloe, did you really push over an elderly woman?" Megan cackled.

"Was she elderly? Shit!"

I couldn't laugh, it would be horrible to, but I couldn't help myself from snickering.

"Right, we need to make sure we're alone, so everyone hold your breath for like a solid second, okay?" I said, before closing my eyes, knife in hand, listening to the noises of the forest around me. I heard every leaf rustle, every branch sway, every gust of wind gently caressing the trees. I heard a twig crack, behind me, about ten steps away, behind a tree. I turned to the tree and threw the knife directly into the bark. I hoped it would scare a fox away or hit something. It did hit something, but just about missed the human hand which curled around the bark.

"Guys get ready, I'm about to get sick of murdering people." I said, grabbing the handgun from my bag and aiming it towards the darkness.

We were far away enough that it was safe to breathe, and finally the gathering had turned into, well, an escape. And I wasn't about to let that fall apart.

Hands. Lights. Flashing. Lights. Hands. Knives. Sirens. Lights. Flashing lights and sirens. Sirens. Siren. Run.

Was I being naïve? Was I acting my age, being an oblivious teenager, not caring about what happens? No. No matter what anyone said, I would survive, my friends would survive, and if that came to me fighting for it, well.

I'm getting ahead of myself, and the sirens were getting too close for comfort. Blaring lights, red and blue, and the stress-inducing sounds of sirens, everything was just too much. While all my friends palely looked into the darkness, where I had saw hands and feet and blue lights reflecting off of the ghostly metal.

The pale beams of moonlight were cast out by the trees, the wind screaming, my friends flinching, bullets flying. I hit one, hit another, hit one more.

"Guys, run that way, run to the houses that way and HIDE." I shouted. It was dark enough no one could see where I was pointing, but Megan knew exactly what I meant. As the others ran in the direction I pointed, she dragged them a completely different way. I knew where she was going. I knew exactly where she was going. The only thing in that direction, was, well the place we first met, and the only hiding spot we had never been found in.

I kept shooting, bullets ripping through soft flesh, screams as I hit them. I hit them. And I felt nothing but relief and adrenaline. The guilt didn't even sink in as I ran, as I took the guns of the fallen, as I took the knives and radios.

I ran towards the iron gates, the iron gates which enclosed my old primary school. Chains and padlocks linked the iron spikes, but there, just ahead was a gap, a gap just big enough to throw my bag through, and just enough space for me to crawl under.

"Guys, guys it's me, where should we go?" I whispered as soon as I saw hooded figures in my old hiding spot, at the bottom of the school field, where the trees and bushes covered the iron gates, and I could sit out of view and hide.

"How did she know to come here?" Ella laughed, thinking we had some psychic connection.

"When Dan used to play hide and seek, he would point the other direction and say he found someone so he could be the person to win, also because I just knew, because you know, I'm cool."

"I mean everyone always does the opposite of what I say, so I figured if you go for boys who I tell you not to, you would go the opposite direction."

"Ouch."
"Yeah, that wasn't funny," I said, throwing a loaded gun Aliyah and Chloe "Sorry."

"It's fine, it's true," She laughed it off before asking "so we have a plan, but how are we going to get to a place lorries go, and what are we going to do after we get on?"

"I already said we can get to the services from the woods..." Aliyah said, before checking if there were bullets in the gun. "Dan, how do you know how to shoot one of these things?"

I took a deep breath before asking Amanda to help make a physical plan. We all decided together we had to find our way into a residential area to hide out until the sirens go away, before Eloise sneezed and said she heard a noise. We all ducked, covered ourselves in brambles and ivy. A faint lawnmower like sound became a harsh, wind-whipping, offensive sound. Searchlights pierced through the forest, the white of the harsh light mixing with the yellow of torches. Glazing over us, we had to remain very still and very quiet. I could just about make out the flashes of sirens in the corner of the forest and hear the radios of the hunters. I could make out what they were saying, something about "ten down" and "blood" and "kill on sight."

One of them had almost seen me, but at the bottom of the brambles was a fence, a fence with a loose panel, a fence that meant we could sneak into the back garden of a residential area, away from the metal bars which kept us inside, and away from the torchlights which almost got us caught.

I whispered to Ella to tell the others when one of us sees the moon in the sky, that we had to run through that panel, and that we had to be quick and quiet. She nodded, and then created the chain. Everyone knew and agreed to the plan, and as soon as Eloise said the word "I see it!" I threw a knife right into a torchlight near us. We had about forty seconds, forty seconds to get as far away from the body.

"Man down!" A hunter screamed, before shooting bullets into the darkness, barely missing us. The shots were loud enough we could run and not be heard. I was the last one through the panel.

"We made it guys!" Eloise said, before pulling us into a group hug.

A light turned on in the upper left window of the house we were in the back garden of. I could almost make out a face from behind the curtains.

"Hold your fucking breath and squeeze behind here!" I hushed, pulling everyone in between the bricks of a garage and the neighbour's house.

"We need to get far away from here, soon." Amanda cried, holding onto my hand tightly.

"I know hun, but we need to wait for the sirens to fade."

"Smart, good plan." Aliyah whispered.

"Excuse me I feel left out from all this planning," Megan grunted, before saying "but okay."

"Yeah Meg, let's just stay out of it." Chloe looked at the handgun in her hand and smiled, and then asked "How do I use this thing?

"It's a semi-automatic, right?" I asked, before she just pressed the gun into my chest."

"Do I look like I know what that means?"

"Okay so keep the safety on, that's this bit, when you're loading, and you just slide this bit to put bullets here and then put it back in, and then pull this bit back and release, got it?"

"Oh, okay yeah, cool, so do I just take the safety off and pull the trigger?"

"Yeah, but aim please." I laughed, handing her the gun back.

"Ah, that's cool, okay." Aliyah said, checking her ammunition and putting the gun into the water bottle holder of her bag.

"Uh, how come they got guns and we didn't?" Eloise asked, from the tone of her voice she was offended.

"Think about it, Eloise you're a vegan and couldn't hurt a fly unless you verbally attacked it, Aliyah has already killed someone and Chloe attacked an old woman to protect herself, and that's just in the last hour, it makes sense to give them the guns first."

"Can we stop bringing it up that I kicked over an old woman?" Chloe laughed.

I almost remember thinking that her instincts were what was going to make us survive.

Dilated Pupils

Aliyah White

Part I:

She has the most incredible eyes.
Twinkling and bright; filled to the brim
with joy. A rare kind of contagious joy.

I look into her eyes and my heart just
wants to burst. Not to mention the colour.
No artist or camera could ever capture the
perfection of her eyes. The warm honey
brown swirling with stunning grassy
green. Little sparks of gold occasionally
peak out through the sea of earthy tones.
And when a glorious ray of sun hits her
face, she's just illuminated. Its unfair how
beautiful she truly is.

And yet, she looks at me. If she wanted, she could easily seduce a model or a millionaire. But she chooses plain old me. Its like a god choosing to love a human. Some days I wake up, I think of her and I'm just overwhelmed with gratitude. And that's just her eyes: I didn't mention her rosy chubby cheeks; or perfectly adorable dimples; the millions of freckles dusted across her nose and face.

The perfect arches of her cupids bow and pouty lips, kissable and soft like a cloud. She is a breath of fresh air, and yet she is mine. What did I do to deserve her?

<u>Part II:</u>

It's the eyes. Perfect almond shape, long jet-black lashes, and adorable smile lines. The colour? Ugh, the colour! Blue but kind of green and a little rim of gold around the pupil. Blessed. That's just what she is. Her genetics just fell perfectly in place to create the most sensational women. They say god handpicked every inch of us. Do I buy that? Not really. But if that were true, he spent a long time creating her. Meticulously adding feature after feature, her blank canvas skin, deep cut cheekbones, and her cute beauty mark right under her left eye.

My constant, ineffable hunger for her is completely insatiable. She notices me. I do not think I'll ever understand why but boy, am I glad she looks my way.

Now I've had a taste of her love, I'm hooked. Addicted. Totally love struck. Cupids arrow has hit me, hit me hard.

Part III:

Lying on the grass with Lila is my new definition of paradise. The sweet aroma of roses gently wafting over us in the crisp breeze. The bright sun providing our serene scene with a warm glow. I can't help but watch her.

Watch her chest rise and fall as she dozes off in my arms. Her glorious crimson curls haphazardly spiralling as if her hair was a flame. Her humble breasts protecting her precious heart from harm.

I wrap my arm around her sleepy form and let her warmth penetrate through me, lighting me up from the inside out. I never want to feel our love go cold. So often love sours, but when I'm with Lila... the whole world around me transforms from a desolate, cold dystopia, to a loving oasis. She is my everything. Her love saved me. She is my soulmate.

We'll always find each-other.

Every life we have, we will share it together.

Patient 65

Aliyah White

Sixty-five. That's me. Patient sixty-five. I knew moving out suddenly with no job and no experience was risky. I anticipated it would be hard. I didn't expect so much to go wrong. And to end up here. Desperate. Poor. And being a guinea pig for scientists testing a new drug. Supposed to enhance the imagination. I have my doubts considering all the shit they made me sign. One of the contracts containing a clause that says if I die, they aren't responsible for my death so anyone I leave behind can't sue them. I don't have a family to care if I die so I signed my life away for a pretty salary. I stay in this hospital wing, get monitored every second of everyday and get paid a hundred pounds per day.

Well, it's been two weeks and I can report I am half-way through this experiment. There's been eight deaths on the wing. Four men, Four women and one child. Not sure which psycho signed their kid up to this but that's not my business. I've also experienced zero symptoms, so I guess I'm not just broken emotionally but physically. They watch me even more than the others. I can't even piss without a million cameras on me. They no longer call me by my name. I'm simply the anomaly. Earlier today, I was informed that they'd be upping my dosage in order to see how much a human can take. So, I imagine I'll be the ninth victim of the drug. They call it Wanderlust. Every victim was a state of mania before passing. The body can only handle so much excitement, I guess.

I'm sat in my bed, staring out the

window when Nurse Ava comes in with

a trolley of Wanderlust. I sit up straight

and stick my arm out. She gently places

my arm down and begins cleaning the

area she'll inject. Applying a numbing

cream. I feel it tingle for a second and

then nothing. Her warm aura is always

a pleasant contrast to the cold,

oppressive glare of cameras. She

flashes me a bright smile before

returning to her trolley. She turns back

to me with a cartoonishly large syringe

needle in hand. Filled with my higher

dosage of Wanderlust. A glowing turquoise liquid.

"Now, I don't want to hurt you Maude, so I need you to keep still" she says. Stuttering slightly. That's when I take notice of the blush on her cheeks.

"You put numbing cream on···You could stab that spot and I wouldn't feel a thing. Say, do I make you nervous Ava? I smile, cockily. Leaning closer to her. She puts the needle down and turns back to me. A fire in her eyes.

"I'm a professional who's been assigned to you. It would be completely unprofessional. But equally, I would be lying if I didn't admit that I admire you".

"Can I take that as a yes, Miss Ava?" I smile. Staring deep into her eyes. She averts her gaze and nods. I sit back and put my arm back where it was. She continues the administration. Filling my arm with the drug. With that, she leaves. My only genuine human connection in years. Nurse Ava.

The day slips away and before I know it, night is upon us. The hospital is quiet and still. A total contrast from the usual chaos of the daytime. I lay down, staring at the ceiling and thinking about her. A few minutes go by of my loving daydream and I begin to feel···odd. My stomach is turning, my head hurts, and I can see flashing lights. Guess this is it.

I wake up, my head rested on the soft pillow of Ava's thighs. She's gently running her fingers through my hair. I sit up sharply, careful not to hit her. Before I can panic, Ava shushes me and tells me to lie back down.

"You're not dead⋯but it looks like you've finally gotten some symptoms. Soon, you may begin feeling different. You may experience delusions, feelings of grandeur, heightened motivation, peak levels of dopamine and upped sex drive. Please tell me whatever you feel. I⋯I don't want anything to happen to you" She explains. I hold up my pinkie and I promise to tell her everything. It all sounds good⋯so how does it end up fatal? Ava helps me up, returning me to my bed and drift off.

I wake up the next day. Feeling unusually perky. I get out of bed feel my body urging me to get active. I open the bed-side table drawer and much to my delight, find a stationary. I lock my door, not wanting to be disturbed. I open the notepad, grab the pen and start writing a story. I haven't written in years, but I suppose, it's always been my thing. That's why failing to get published completely killed me.

A few minutes go by, I turn the light on. The sun has set, and I'm still wrapped up in my work. Beginning a manuscript for a novel. I look down at my page and the words slowly peel off the page and fill my cramped hospital room.

Paragraphs form together and I see my story come together. Literally. There's the protagonist, Emma! Just as I imagined her, standing two feet away from me! Beside her is her love interest, Kai! They begin to play out every moment I imagined. I become so enthralled by my own work, I hardly notice the sun rising for the third time today. That's when my show is interrupted by the door crashing to the ground. Emma, Kai and I spin around to see several doctors and a visibly distressed Ava. Emma and kai turn back into words and return to the page. It's ruined···It was all coming together! My dream···and they ruined it. The world returns to being cold and empty. I look down and, on the page, my story is gone. Replaced my big bold letters.

Kill them. Love Emma.

Emma? Now I'm talking to my characters. If I do her bidding, maybe she'll come back. I can't lose her! My dream can come true, my life won't be meaningless, my parents will want me back when they see how successful I am, and I can use the money to pay for a wedding when I finally propose to Ava. Those white coats already have it all. They're preying on desperate sad people and can't even call me my name.

"Anomaly, you need to be moved. The drug is taking effect" Doctor Whittaker states. His colleagues walk over and grab my manuscript. I scream and beg for them to give it back, but they refuse. Blunt. Cold. Heartless. I fall to my knees. Totally ruined. That's when under the bed, I notice a butterknife and a smiling Emma.

"Ava⋯. Run!" I shout before plunging the blade into Doctor Whittaker. Pulling out his puny heart. I hear a few shrieks echo out. The man holding my manuscript cautiously walks past me and places it on the bed. I move to put the knife down, but Emma stops me.

"NOT GOOD ENOUGH MAUDE!" she yells. I nod. I walk behind my bed and approach the quivering man. I stab his eyes out. It's kinda funny. I feel raucous laughter erupt out of me. Those bastards wanted to stop my dream from manifesting and now they're paying for it. And if they never made that drug, this would have never happened. I would have stayed miserable, unmotivated and useless. I turn to off the rest of them, but they've all escaped. And Ava is there. Staring at me. Mortified. Why is she angry? Doesn't she see? If I don't, Emma will leave, and I won't have anything to offer. I'll be invisible again···she's crying? Why? I don't understand!

I wake up. Damp. Cold. I take in my surroundings and realise where I am. My hospital room. I'm covered in Dr Whittaker's blood. The precious pages of my manuscript cover the room. Soaked in his blood.

"You promised you'd tell me Maude. You killed Dr Whittaker and for what?" I hear Ava's voice blast through the room.

"Emma···Emma told me to. But they tried to take my manuscript! It's my everything. My purpose. It will fix everything!" I respond excited.

"Maude···you're gone. Completely. You killed a man. An innocent man. A pioneer in the field"

"Whittaker? I didn't kill him! I just thought he was being heartless so···isn't kinda funny? I took away his heart but it's almost a joke!" I begin to chuckle to myself.

"No. It's not. And to think I almost loved you···Goodbye Maude. You will be going away for a long time".

And that's when it stopped. I never heard Ava's voice ever again. Ava's gone. Emma is gone. Kai is gone. My money is gone. My manuscript has been destroyed. It's all gone. I'm gone. Patient 65. The anomaly. It's all dead.

The drug may not have killed me. But I wish it had.

Mirror

Aliyah White

I'm making my way up the winding

stairs leading to the top of the house.

My hand sliding up the rail as dust is

catapulted into the air. A few coughs

and many steps later, I reach for the

golden handle. In one motion, I grip the

edges of the opening and hoist myself

up. Using whatever core muscle, I can.

Once my feet hit the ground, I straighten

up and place my hands on my hips.

The attic.

It's not often that I come here. The several flights of stairs requiring more energy than I can typically muster. And the lack of ladder making it even harder to access. But we're going through his stuff. Maybe donating it, finding some family heirlooms perhaps? I'm not excited. It's going to be an all too painful reminder of how incredible he was. But it must be done. I press on, slowly venturing deeper into the loft. A smile creeps onto my flushed face as I take in the antique wasteland in front of me. That's when I notice exactly what I'm looking for. The mouldy cardboard box labelled 'Baby boy'. Mum said it's full to the brim of Jackson memorabilia. Dating back to before I was even born. Upon opening the box, tears prick up in my eyes. Hands quivering and heart breaking. The cutest collection of old pictures, toys and clothes. It's nostalgic but painful. I begin to rummage, pushing through the onset of emotion. His toddler days just break my heart. Little did we know then of the tragedy that would occur. All the potential lost to one disease. I snap my head away, unable to bear anymore. Despite only

taking in one cardigan and two pictures.

As my head snaps, I notice something

odd. A box. But unlike all the other

boxes, this one is wooden. The lid

covered in beautiful intricate carvings.

Spiralling paisley patterns. The

mesmerising design fills me to the brim

with curiosity. I place my hand on the

lid, softly to avoid putting getting a

splinter. But to my surprise, it's perfectly

smooth. I tip the box and discover a

keyhole. Its odd shape making it

blatantly obvious which key will open its

secrets. The very key around my neck. I thought it was just a pendant this whole time. I guess Jackson wanted me to find this box and that's why he slipped this into my palm on his death bed. The memory haunts me. His weak self on that bed, desperately gripping to life. It's all too much. I put the box down, wipe some stray tears away and breathe. I gather my bearings and pull the necklace off. Gripping the key in my shaking hands and daring to open the box. I hear a click, indicating that my suspicions were correct. I open the lid and inside is a note and a beautiful hand-held mirror. It seems to be made of pure gold, the design is etchings of vines, roses and birds. It's stunning but why this? I open the folded parchment and realise the note is written in his hand. It reads: Dear sister, I fear that you reading this meets I've met a grim fate. But I wanted to leave you a gift. To reflect on our precious memories. Of course, that's bad a joke. Forgive me, I am sick while writing this. But I miss you greatly I'm sure and I love you dearly. I saw this at the market and knew you'd love it. Enjoy this parting gift. Your loving brother, Jackson.

I take a pause. His jokes are awful, but his taste is exquisite. I hold up the mirror and the reflection shocks me so greatly; I almost drop the thing. I'm sitting in the attic. Wearing a simple blue dress with an apron on top. But in the mirror, it looks like I'm in a castle made of diamonds. The definition of opulence. My hair is ornate, and my dress is shimmery like the ocean in sunlight. I check my surroundings and sanity. The mirror is somehow manipulating its own reflection in real-time. Fascinating! I grab the mirror and go to share its trickery with mother. But as I move, my castle disappears. I jump down from the attic and check the reflection. Inside the mirror, my hallway is transformed into a lazy river. I'm stood on a humongous rock and flowing by are millions of salmon. My nose even deceives me: the scent of salt surrounding me. The absurdity of my circumstance makes me laugh like a hyena. How is this even possible?

Jackson, you son of a gun, when I someday

come to meet you in the great beyond; I will have to bombard you with questions. How has he managed this? That's when I'm reminded of reality. I'm not a princess or an explorer. I am a simple girl. And Jackson is long gone. I drag myself back to my bedroom, hugging my knees to my chest, I gently sob. Drowned in utter sadness and filled with hopelessness. Jackson···

A few minutes of my pathetic tears roll on and I eventually pick up the mirror again. But to my horror, the reflection is not another pleasant scene. It's mortifying. I'm sat on a throne made of bones, surrounded by roaring flames and my eyes are bleeding! To my right, Beelzebub himself places a hand on my shoulder. His face obscured by darkness but his teeth peek through. He shines a diabolical smirk. I scream and drop the mirror. Thankfully, it lands behind me on the bed. Safe from shattering. A world distorting mirror has no business being in my possession. Especially when it appears to be influenced by emotion. I lug myself back into the attic, placing the mirror gently in its box and closing the lid. I hold onto the note though. I can handle that much. I lock it up and hide it in a far corner. Descending once again and running to my bedroom. I collapse onto my bed and find myself in prayer.

"Dear God. Please tell Jackson I appreciate his gift, but it's bewitched. Therefore, I've returned it to its box. But I love him. I hope he's resting well. And if that vision of Satan gives me nightmares, I won't forgive him" I chuckle. Unconsciously speaking my prayer out loud attracts mother's attention.

"Darling? Who are you talking to?" She calls from the hallway.

"God! I'm not crazy!" I announce back. I hear the door open and sit up. Mother walks in and gives me a tight hug. We all miss him bitterly. But I should focus on the positive. I still have Mother; Father and I am still an auntie despite Jackson's passing. The world is full of things to be grateful for. I don't need that peculiar mirror to whisk me away.

Eivor the Undying

Rowan Costen

Usually, immortals get bored of life after the first few centuries or so. They wish for relief, for something more, for a way to move on. Many immortals that think this way walk our earth: angels, deities, certain species of fae, etc. They all share something in common: that boredom that comes like a sickness and refuses to leave, infecting all that you once enjoyed, ruining any pleasure life may once have held. Eivor was not one of these immortals. In fact, they never have been.

Eivor is a vampire. But don't worry, they're actually quite a nice vampire, and the truth is, they'd never hurt a fly. In this day and age, it was rare to find a vampire, and rarer still to find one that would hurt you. You see, vampires are one of the few types of immortals that can still be killed in some way, and thus most of them are gone. If they choose to hurt people based on who they are, they will be hunted down and most likely murdered. If they choose not to hurt people, they die because they have no food. If they do not die from either of these, they go out fighting each other (for fun, no less!) Eivor was different.

Yes, it sounds cliché, so I'm not going to give you the whole 'they're not like other vampires' spiel. But truthfully, they weren't.

Eivor had found other ways to survive all these centuries. They took a course in medicine and learnt how to draw blood with a syringe, found willing donors who would help them in return for payment or a simple favour. Before that was possible, they would live on animals as far as they could, and when they were forced to take blood from humans, they took from the freshly dead. Eivor had always been considered a little eccentric in the immortal community, but others respected them for how unwilling they were to harm a human being, and mostly left them to themself. Of course, there were those that mocked them for their ideologies (imagine it, a vampire with a conscience, a soul. What a fool, they would whisper behind Eivor's back). But Eivor just carried on being who they were, no matter what, and that is what earned them respect.

Throughout the centuries, Eivor's misadventures had become infamous, the stuff of legend. You see, they were a rather unfortunate vampire, and often found themself in situations that were unbecoming of an immortal of their stature.

When asked what it was like to see the pyramids built, Eivor would tell you "I've no idea. I was a two-year-old child in South Africa at the time." They were born with a gift from the gods, an immortal no matter what, yet they still managed to miss anything interesting across the next few centuries. They had been curious, but it was the kind of childish curiosity that made you care a lot about the little things, like the funny-looking pebble at the end of your garden, and that made you not care at all about the big things, like climate

change, politics and history being made.

When asked about the Greek and

Roman empires, they would simply

smile a sad smile and shake their head

a little, unwilling to admit that they had

been turned near the beginning of the

ancient Greeks' era, and took a

depression nap through the next near-

millennia, forcing themself to remain in

perpetual sleep for fear of hurting

anyone. Fleeing because you don't want

to cause harm is honour; fleeing

because you don't want to be harmed is

cowardice. This is what Eivor told

themself all these years, that they were

doing it right because of this. Doing

what right, they never quite worked out.

Life, they supposed, or Unlife,

depending on your perspective.

When asked how the Renaissance was,

Eivor would roar with laughter about the

time they fell down a hole in Scotland,

and were thought to be an enchanted

well for two hundred years. By the time

anyone was kind enough to pull them

out, they were starving, beyond pissed, and the renaissance was over.

When asked to describe the industrial revolution, they would chuckle a little and glance at the floor, as though embarrassed, not by themself, but by humanity, for considering the 1800s as an era of industrial revolution, when he had been in his home, south Africa, helping to clear up the terrible mess left behind for the Xhosa tribesmen after the Cape Frontier Wars. A society left to fend for itself when the rest of the world moved on, deciding that it wasn't worth their time. What a shame.

When asked what they thought, based on past experience, would be the turning point of the present, for better or for worse, Eivor would generally not tell you anything political, or anything scientific, nothing social or economic. They still didn't really care for all that, still consumed with that childlike curiosity that told them what really mattered. They would mutter exasperatedly to themself for a moment, before settling on the arts. Books, films, modern technology like the phone or computer. Eivor thought all that stuff is what would change the future. Such a shame nobody listened to them. Perhaps if they had, they could have stopped it...

That said, Eivor was not the dreary, cynical, world-weary sort of immortal you'd think them to be. They were optimistic, naïve even, not for the future, but for the people all around them. They enjoyed everything they did with vigour, a passion for the worldly that was bordering on hedonism. They romanticised all the little things in life, a bird chanting its morning song from a willow tree, a gold and grey sunset that appeared every night or so, a dog yapping excitedly at its owner as it chased a ball every morning. In Eivor's opinion, if their life had to be eternal, they might as well enjoy that eternity.

In fact, when asked how any period of history, or indeed the present was for them, Eivor would probably tell you the exact opposite of what you wanted to hear. Not just because they were that kind of person - stubborn, contrary and full of a sort of loving bitterness for the world - but because they had seen life for what it really was, not what history had made it out to be.

It wasn't often that Eivor got involved in the true course of history; he preferred to watch the important events from afar if he even could be bothered to watch them at all. Rather than do what so many of the immortals that were now dead had done, watching the ups and downs of the ages, influencing where they could and teaching what had really happened where they couldn't, Eivor had actually found themself a hobby.

They were a thrill seeker, plain and simple. If they couldn't die from natural causes, they figured they should have a bit of fun with it. They learnt to skydive, taking lessons once a week until confident they could do it alone. It was the best feeling in the world, thought Eivor, to soar the skies like a peaceful dove, observing its beauty from afar.

The elation that followed you for hours afterwards was worth the thrill of danger and rush of adrenaline a hundred times over. They learnt to forge their own weapons and tools from any metal that couldn't harm them (and sometimes those that could), becoming part of the forge as the metal and flames hummed to the beat of their soul. They were going to change the world with their new skills, and around them, the world burned.

Well, not literally burned, but it may as well have done. You may be thinking in this dangerous moment of the Amazon being brought to the ground by the fire of mere humans who fancy themselves as wrathful gods. Or perhaps your mind brought you to the Notre-dame fire, a relic of beautiful history, bloodied and destroyed. Maybe there has been a fire in your life, one that left you ruined and desperate, wanting and alone. But you see, fire doesn't have to be literal; fire can be anything that holds a passion behind it, bright, beautiful, burning.

Around Eivor, yes, the world did burn,

but the flame was a bright new star,

and the world was all the better for it.

But how can you burn something and

expect it not to eventually be destroyed?

Candles are supposed to burn,

providing heat and light for those who

desire it, but eventually it will run dry,

splutter out, and perish. Perhaps Eivor

did make things better for a while, but

they weren't even close to the end of

suffering, and what they did served only

to bring about a far worse era.

You could perhaps call Eivor the

Prometheus of their age; their flame

burned brighter than a thousand suns,

their voice sweeter than the nectar of

the gods, but all the while their hands

were outstretched for the stars, they

and the world were severely punished

for it. They brought knowledge, yes:

infinite knowledge, dangerous

knowledge, forbidden knowledge; Eivor

brought knowledge of the future.

At first, it seemed magical, divine, ethereal. Eivor spent decades searching for anybody with the sight, anybody with knowledge of what was to come. Perhaps he found the special somebody. Perhaps they never did. In what would come to pass, it would not matter.

They learnt how to enter a dream-trance, and how to search the world through this. They could spend days at a time in such a trance, poring over the world that seemed laid out before them like a map. Indeed, they would map anything that they saw in their trance, handing out the papers when it was over to anybody that would so much as glance in their general direction. The future was bright. It seemed like a happily ever after to the people that Eivor helped. They could tell anybody where they should and shouldn't be, what would help and what would hinder their lives' journeys, and all they needed to do was ask.

Following through on their earlier passions, Eivor eventually digitised his entire business. His maps were laid out as lines of code - tags and comments on the locations of the world, on people and places, animals and things. Even the abstract was carefully considered and written about in Eivor's work. Unfortunately, this breakthrough was also when they began to slip into nightmare trance.

Piercing blue eyes would haunt Eivor from the darker corners of the world, the ones they hardly dared visit to map out. The same curiosity that consumed

Eivor themself was recognisable in those eyes, moulding them as soft and harsh all at once. Those eyes had such power, such icy intensity, burning into Eivor as they worked. As though their owner was searching for something.

It seemed in the days that followed, the eyes had infiltrated everybody's maps, everybody's dreams. People were afraid to sleep, and further afraid to check their phones. Friends were lost, people were dropping like flies, their spirits once as high as the sun now plummeting down to Earth, hopeful

wings melted and singed around the

edges. Eivor couldn't get a minute's

peace. The clouding smoke that always

follows a bright bonfire began to

consume at least Eivor's little corner of

the world. People were begging them

for help, to make it stop, to make it go

away, at every moment, and still those

eyes haunted their nightmares, awake

or asleep.

That is, until it stopped. One day, as

though the embers had finally sputtered

out, the eyes departed, along with

everything else. After decades upon

decades of searching for the sight, they

had lost it all. People were ruined,

desperate, blind. Not only to what was

to come, but to what was happening in

the present. In the years that followed, it

became known as the Great Blinding,

for it affected everybody in Eivor's

homelands. All at once, their world

became helpless, desolate, abandoned.

Though they couldn't be seen anymore,

Eivor felt as exposed as one of their

maps. It was as though those eyes were still there, rounded and excitable, but wild, and far from kind, stripping Eivor down to the essence of their future. It was weeks before that stopped too; Eivor supposed his future was rather a long one. Perhaps this mysterious person had found what they were looking for, or perhaps they had given up on Eivor and decided they weren't worth the time.

Whatever had happened, Eivor was left with no clients, no ideas, no knowledge;

alone, anxious, afraid. Indeed, all that remained in Eivor's once brilliant mind, beyond the blackened smoke that tainted his vision, were two words.

Two words that would change everything. Two words that would bring the world to either darkness or to light. Two words, which they would hear without pause for breath for decades on end.

"The Seeker."

Eye of the Storm: Journey through the Ages

Rowan Costen

Silence. It's that first moment after a question is asked, a mistake is made, a box is opened. It's that agonising second between the light and the dark, the pride and the Fall, where you know you're being cast out, but can't even begin to fathom what comes next. It's that space between, where all the darkness of the world is revealed, but Hope cannot yet be seen.

The raging winds beat down on the once vibrant forest with the force of a thousand gales; it sapped all life from the ancient trees that once burst with flashes of frosted silver and cool amber. The river Morai no longer whispered with the voice of Hecate's secrets. Now the harsh winter chained and held back its beauty as ice forked across it. Pounding the river's surface, a blizzard penetrated the usual idyllic peace of the forest, reaching its source and tearing it apart from the inside. A pool at the edge of the clearing had frozen over, bringing the storm to an abrupt halt. No settlement stood here, for all should be peaceful — and yet somehow it was not.

Around the pond, clusters of quartz and selenite had bloomed, sprouting from the life-giving spring of the river Morai. They no longer twinkled with a kind winter's light; they had turned dull and grey, shattering into stormy shards. The whole clearing vibrated with frequencies that just seemed wrong, as though somebody had reversed the polarity of nature.

I suppose you could say that somebody had reversed the polarity of nature, and that somebody was me. Devastated, I sat by a tree stump run around by hundreds of rings. I was entangled in a faint endeavour to repair the damage of this terrible storm. Unfortunately, it was as futile as my desperate cries for help, carried away with the harsh screaming of the gale. There was nothing that could be done. It was what I had been warned of from the start, the price of a breakthrough. Hope had been set free, but at what cost?

Legend of the Lotus

Rowan Costen

A *Temple of Roses* Short Story.

Not all tragedy is fatal. Sometimes, tragedy can be comforting; sometimes, tragedy is home. Or rather, when your home is no longer safe, tragedy is all you have left, it welcomes you with open arms, and you are quite happy to receive its embrace.

Some stories never end. They drift through space and time, searching for an anchor to keep them alive. One such story is a tale that has been discredited by philosophers and historians alike, the tale of a goddess that came far too late. One such story is the tale of Mesperyian.

We all know how that story goes. A love goddess, spurned by jealousy and foolish anger, seeks to destroy the livelihood of a naive young girl, forever tearing her from her family and her destiny. We've all read Psyche and Eros, it's not an unfamiliar tale. But Mesperyian surfaced a lot later than the old myths, a creation of the modern age, rather than her ancient counterparts. That's not to say it shouldn't be treated in the same way.

For is a myth not just a story created to explain parts of nature? And is a deity not just a figure created by the world as something to believe in?

But that is not what this tale is about. Indeed, this tale takes place a little after the first cycle of seasons, after Mesperyian was forced out of her underworld home to wander the mortal realms forever. She was a curious young soul, and after everything that had happened to her, she had vowed to help as much of the mortal world as she could, through her affinity for giving nature a helping hand.

On her travels, the young goddess came across a barren island, desolate and abandoned, no sign of life anywhere around. A stream meandered through the heart of the island, though its milky-white waters bore none of the life-giving properties that a river should. Mesperyian knelt down by the river and cupped a little of its water in her hands, hoping to cool herself down a little. As she touched the water, however, she felt the memory of her broken home and failed battle begin to fade, and dropped the water in horror. This had to be where the river Lethe let out from the depths. She didn't like to think about what would happen if mortals came across this place, though she did find that the pain of her hardships had faded a little.

How wonderful it would be, she thought, if she could use this to aid those who had also felt such pain and failed such battles. Without really thinking about what she was doing, the goddess was weaving the milky waters into the shape of flowers. Lotus flowers.

"There," she smiled at her work, lotus plants adorning every bank of the river, knowing that if anybody passed through here, the flowers would prevent them from falling into the river. And, being made from Lethe water, these lotuses held the power to reduce pain, bring happiness and reduce stress. Any mortal who found this place would never want for anything else, Mesperyian was sure of it.

Unfortunately, she was right. I'll spare you the details. If you want to know what happened on that island, go read the

Odyssey. That story has already been told. But Mesperyian's story kept drifting, until it found somewhere else to dock itself. She had 'helped' one island already. Time would only tell where she would go next. The temple of roses holds many secrets; the stars only know what we shall find there in the future.

The Island Initiative

A continuation of

Project LXCII from

Misfortune

By Rowan Costen

Part 2: The Guardian Angels

"Right," Sara said to herself, trying to get used to the sound of her own voice again. She pulled her hair back into a ponytail, tying it with the band she always kept around her wrist. "This island isn't very big. I should find the highest point and-"

She didn't have much time to worry about what she would do when she got there, because almost immediately, a group of nine people came rushing towards her. Actual, human people. She could hardly believe her eyes.

"It's you!" The one at the head of the group said. "They told us you would come. Oh, it's so wonderful to see you!"

"Stella," an older-sounding woman chided from further back. "The poor girl just got here. Give her some space."

"Uh, hello? Who are you, exactly, and what am I doing here?" Sara was relieved to see other survivors, but the girl's enthusiastic greeting had startled her a little, and there was something··· off about these people.

"I am Tatiana Thorpe," the older woman said, stepping forward. "And these," she gestured to the group. Well, these are my guardian angels."

They all waved at her from behind Ms Thorpe. Sara felt a little overwhelmed. She hadn't interacted with another human since she turned Max away from her door back home. She wondered what had become of him. There was no way he could have survived the swarm. Suddenly, she felt a little guilty. Perhaps if she had let him in that day, things would have been different. He could have been spared.

As if reading her thoughts, Ms Thorpe took her hand and said, "don't worry, love. You'll fit right in here. No need to dwell on the past." She smiled comfortingly, gesturing to the *guardian angels* as she had called them, to come forward. "I don't expect you to remember everybody right away, but in time you will get to know my dear children. Let me introduce you," they all lined up in a row. "This is Opal, Ignis, Lilith, Stella, Flora, Xiva, Darryl and Delta. Each of them is in charge of a different aspect of the island. Together, it is our job to create a haven in which humanity might thrive once more. You can be a part of that too, if you would like. What do you say?"

Everybody smiled and nodded encouragingly. Sara wasn't sure what to say. It would be a lot of responsibility. But she did like the thought of finally giving back to the world that had raised her, and Ms Thorpe had been ever so kind to her since she arrived.

"What do I say?" Sara looked around apprehensively, finally making a decision. "I would be honoured to be a part of this."

"Excellent," Ms Thorpe said. The guardian angels all cheered and high-fived one another. They seemed like such a tight-knit group, Sara couldn't help but wonder if she would ever fit in. But at the very least, they all seemed to like her, and she had a good feeling about them too. "Then I now pronounce you a guardian angel. Welcome aboard!"

"Thank you," Sara said. "I have a question though. What did-" She hesitated for a moment, trying to remember the girl's name. "What did Stella mean when she said *they told us you would come*? I don't mean to be rude, it's just that-"

"Oh it's no worry at all dear. The creatures who brought you here have been inhabitants of this island for centuries. I stumbled across this place one day in my youth, and always hoped to make a home out of it. Over time, I have accumulated quite a crew of people like you - people who have been displaced from their home by any number of disasters. They speak sometimes, the creatures. Not many can understand their words, but some time ago, they told me that the last guardian would come when the end arrived. I never knew what it meant until recently, when the creatures came out of their hibernation. Now that you are here, I know what this island is truly meant for. Finally, The Initiative can begin."

"Right," Sara said slowly. She hadn't really understood any of that, but she nodded politely, figuring that she would learn in time.

"Oh, we should assign you a project. Almost everyone here has one. I have just the thing for you! Since you have bonded so well with the creatures, I think it would be wonderful if you could care for them. Keep them out of harm's way, make sure they are comfortable. Listen when they speak, make note of the future that they tell. What shall we call your project, dear?"

Sara thought for a moment. "Project LCXII" she pronounced it 'LC-12.' Remembering the dream she had that kicked off all of this, she thought that *long count twelve* made the most sense. She looked at the group for approval. Everybody was smiling and nodding along. Ms Thorpe took her hand and led her to the rest of the guardians, who immediately wrapped her in a group hug. Though she didn't usually enjoy affection like this, she did miss being in contact with other humans, and it was so wonderful to be appreciated for once.

"Let's get you some supplies," Stella stepped forward as they all pulled away from each other. "Come with me to the Port and Basecamp. We can grab some food, water and clothes for you, then I'll show you to your bunk."

"Thanks," Sara smiled gratefully, looking down at her tattered clothes. She was still wearing what she had on weeks ago, when the swarm first came to her town. Her leggings, while practical for walking, had been ripped practically to shreds by the metallic hide of the creature. Her shirt was singed in multiple places from the initial attacks.

Port and Basecamp was an interesting place. It consisted of a huge dome, which contained two large storage rooms, one for food and one for other supplies, as well as a security centre with screens that displayed different areas of the island, and some photos of the guardians on the walls. The dome was connected to a bridge, which led to a small stretch of land that seemed to be completely abandoned, aside from a collection of huge shipping containers. They were stacked on top of each other in such a way that they almost looked like a building.

Sara didn't have much time to address the odd container-building though; Stella dragged her excitedly into the supply store.

"I think we have just the thing for you," she said, digging around in some crates in the back of the room. It was a huge place, thought Sara as she waited for Stella to return with her new clothes. She wondered who had built this dome, and why, but was quickly pulled out of her musings when Stella tapped her on the shoulder.

"Here!" she proclaimed, thrusting a pile of material into Sara's hands. "It gets really hot on the island, so I figured that this would be the perfect mix of practical and cool."

Sara unfolded the clothes, to discover an olive green crop top, embroidered with a pair of wings and a halo. She noticed that Stella had that symbol too, and wondered if all the guardians wore it. She then unfolded a pair of leggings, much like the ones that she was wearing, except they were dark grey and had a pattern of vines climbing up one leg. There was a slit across each knee.

"Well?" Stella said expectantly. "Go try them on," Sara just looked at her. "Oh, right, you don't know where to change. To the right of the other store room, down the stairs," she pointed her in the right direction.

Within a few minutes, Sara was back, and was greeted by all the rest of the guardians, minus Ms Thorpe.

"Perfect!" Stella cried, throwing her arms around Sara. She thought about pushing her away, blushing a little, but decided it would be easier and more polite just to accept the hug.

"Well, almost," one of the other women said. She had pale skin and black hair that was completely shaved on one side. Sara wondered if she was wearing contacts, or if her eyes were just naturally red. She whispered something to Stella, who dove back into the store room to retrieve something else.

When she got back, she handed Sara a cap. It was light grey with a black rim, and had some sort of symbol stitched across the front. A downwards-pointing triangle with a stroke through the centre, sort of like a letter A on its head.

"Now it's perfect," the red-eyed girl nodded approvingly. Everybody else murmured their assent.

"Ms Thorpe told us to walk you back to the dorms," one of the other guardians said. "She probably didn't want you left alone with Stella too long," they laughed, and for a moment, Sara looked a little offended on Stella's behalf, then Stella started laughing too, and soon all nine of them were in fits of laughter, all clutching onto each other for balance.

Though Sara had only been a part of the Island Initiative for a few hours, she felt as though she had been there all her life. Though she hadn't known them for very long, she really felt as though she belonged with the guardian angels.

Part 3: Project Odyssey

Sara spent a lot of her time on the island helping out the other guardians. There wasn't much for her to do up at the north point, where her swarm had settled. Sure, the creatures needed oiling occasionally, and she had to listen out for the rare times when their odd clicking language actually meant something, but more often than no, there was nothing for her to do.

On this particular day, she was working with Opal, down in the lost city. This area of the island might have been a real civilisation once, with living and social spaces, but it would have been many thousands of years ago. Now, all that was left of the ancient city was ruins and vines. When the whole place came crumbling down, nature moved back in, taking over the ruins until they were completely irreparable. That is, until Opal came along.

Opal was the oldest of the guardian angels, the first to arrive after Ms Thorpe had settled on the island. Her eyes were two different colours - one silver, one gold - like the sun and the moon. A constellation of silvery freckles adorned her dark skin. Her hair was a deep blue hue. Like everybody else, she had a pair of wings and a halo embroidered on her clothes. For her, this was a delicate robe in sky blue, a satin apron with red and silver accents tied around her waist. Sara thought that she had quite a motherly presence. She was soft-spoken and patient, with an accent that she just couldn't quite place.

Sara discovered that Opal was in charge of project Odyssey. She had a certain way of communing with nature, and had been slowly working back the vines that had woven their way through the civilisation since she arrived. Apparently, the aim was to make the space livable again, in such a way that it hadn't been in thousands of years. Once the world was habitable once more, the people would need a place to stay, and they couldn't very well squeeze everybody into the shipping-container bunks of the guardians.

Once the network of trees and vines had been pushed back out of the city, Opal had been tasked with physically rebuilding the city. This was particularly daunting to her - though she was good with plants and the environment, she had never actually *built* anything before. That was where Sara came in. She was good with her hands, and even better at following instructions. If she could get a hold of the materials, she would be more than happy to help restore this lost city.

Sara approached Opal in her city one day, looking for odd-jobs that she could fulfil across the island. Without even turning around to face her, the woman said,

"Libra. April 30th 2012. There's no need to play the martyr, although you may feel like one lately. If you feel like you've been tied down to a thousand obligations, perhaps you ought to take a step back and reevaluate."

Sara did just that, taking a literal step back from Opal. "Uh, thanks?" She said. "I just came by to see if you wanted any help."

"Sorry, dear," Opal turned around and smiled. "I did not want to frighten you. The stars thought you should know that."

"Oh," Sara said, not so reassured. Nevertheless, she sat down on the ground next to where Opal had been working her magic. Perhaps the older guardian was right - perhaps it was time Sara took a step back from the darkness and the danger and this crazy new world that she had been thrown into.

"What do you do, to get away from it all?" Sara looked uncertainly at Opal, turning to face her so that they were sitting cross-legged, looking into each others' eyes.

"I look to the stars," Opal responded simply, turning her gaze skyward. "Project Odyssey is a noble cause, but it is truly colossal. Oftentimes, it is all too much for my little heart. I do not know what comes next, or if this project will ever come to completion. The one thing that I do know, is that the stars are always there. Though they move and change with each day and night, they are constant and forever. The stars are my solace." Even though it was light out, Opal looked contentedly at the cosmos, as if she could see it all mapped out before her. Sara wasn't sure what to make of the older woman's advice. She didn't even understand all of the words that she had said, but Opal always seemed so serene. Perhaps she ought to at least try.

And so, she copied Opal's stance, turning to face the sky, but was met with only blinding sunlight. She winced, lowering her eyes to the ground. There had to be another way.

"It is ok, child," Opal placed her hand beneath Sara's chin, tilting her head up so that they were looking into each other's eyes once again. "There are many ways to escape this world. Perhaps the stars are not meant for you. I think, you should talk to Ignis."

"But··· what about Project Odyssey?" Sara protested

"We have many years to complete this project. There is only one today."

"Okay," Sara said uncertainly; it sounded more like a question than an answer. "Ignis··· They're the one with the volcano, right?"

"Indeed," Opal nodded. "Project Calypso. Fare thee well, child."

"Uh, thank you. I think," Sara quickly realised that she wasn't going to get a straight answer out of Opal any time soon, so she did as she was told and

went to visit Ignis.

Part 4: Project Calypso

Sara had never seen anything quite like the jungle. It was a dense canopy of lush green leaves and tropical palms. The canopies were rife with birdsong, and there was a distant yet constant hum, as though something huge under the earth was shifting. It always smelled like rainfall and flowers, and the air was thick with humidity. Sara was exceedingly confused about how such a tiny island could contain so many different climates. I mean, Sara thought, they had only travelled a short distance from England's coastline. There was no way that this was natural.

Ignis was nowhere to be found. Sara might have stumbled around the jungle for hours, searching for the inferno that raged at its heart. She assumed that was where Ignis would be - working to keep the volcano from consuming any more of the jungle than it already had. That was what project Calypso was all about - restoring the jungle. Nature and its many ecosystems are some of the most important things on the planet for sustaining all forms of life - humans included. If they planned to make this place habitable for other survivors, it first had to be habitable for the forces of nature.

Sara realised she had taken a wrong turn when she came across a river. A rather small river, mind, but a river nonetheless. It might have been called a stream, or a creek. Perhaps that was where the old creek town got its name. It was an impressive monument to nature though, rushing whitewater rapids cutting a swift and elegant path through the landscape. Sara wondered if maybe this was the way for her to *escape* as it were. She would simply stay here and admire the forces of nature that Ignis fought to protect.

The sound of the water drowned out almost everything else, filling Sara's head and bringing her to an innate sense of calm that she simply could not achieve at the northern point. Indeed, the water was so loud as it rushed by, that Sara nearly jumped out of her skin when she felt a sharp clap on her back.

"Ignis!" She cried. "You startled me."

Not acknowledging Sara's outcry, they said. "Caught up in the river, eh?" they looked at Sara, with a strange sort of concern, as though she was in danger. "It can be quite entrancing. It must like you, to spare your life - others have been so drawn to the creek that they jump in and get swept up by the currents. Like that old legend, y'know-"

"The sirens," Sara finished for her, shuddering at the thought of what could have been. The river no longer seemed like a calming presence - instead it was a cold current of cruelty, just waiting for the moment to strike out and bring her to her doom.

"Well, best not to dwell on it!" Ignis took Sara's arm and guided her back into the heart of the jungle. "I swear this place needs its own guardian," she shook her head, looking thoughtfully back at the river they had left behind.

Ignis was an interesting guardian, Sara thought. Much like Opal, there was something a little off about them, as though they weren't quite human. Their eyes, which Sara had thought were simply brown at first, had a golden glow to them that burned like fire from within. Like Opal, they had a certain way with nature, but it was so fundamentally different. Rather than communing with the jungle to build it back to life, they seemed to be working to hold back the inferno itself - they seemed to be able to control the raging fire.

Sara had to admit that she was a little scared of Ignis. While they acted friendly enough, they were quite blunt and rough around the edges. There was a certain warmth about them, a welcoming feeling, but Sara got the sense that if they wanted to, that warmth could grow and it could burn. They didn't speak much, preferring to communicate through actions rather than words. What little they did say was often without tact. They got on well with the other guardians though - one could say like a house on fire. There was a certain dynamic between all of the guardians, all of them working as one unit despite their differences. Even Sara, the newest guardian, had felt immediately accepted into that unit, becoming part of the team in the blink of an eye. If everyone else could learn to understand Ignis's way of communicating, thought Sara, then she could too.

Watching Ignis carefully as they picked their way through roots and leaves, Sara made sure to copy their steps exactly, picking up the tiniest details of their movements. The jungle was a treacherous place. Sara had to stop several times to free her hair from loose branches, and she began to understand why Ignis kept theirs cropped so short. Even pulled back in a ponytail, Sara's long hair was becoming a safety hazard. The sun filtered gently through the trees, yet somehow the heat and humidity was intense. Ignis's dark skin gleamed in the light, dotted with burn scars from working in the constant heat. Neither said a word to the other as they walked, simply focussing on not tripping over various roots and leaves, until Sara realised she could hear the low hum of the volcano again, and stopped abruptly.

"Ignis?" She asked tentatively. "What do you do to get away from it all - y'know, when you've been working at the volcano for hours and you need to just let go?"

"I-" Ignis faltered for the first time since she set foot in the jungle. "Well, I don't really. Project Calypso is a full time job. It takes top priority in my life, as every guardian's project should. I suppose I do like to work in the forge beneath the mountain, making new supplies for the survivors, but really that's part of the project. Fire's a destructive force. I have to focus completely on keeping back the volcano."

"But don't you get overwhelmed?" Sara asked.

"Of course," Ignis responded. "But that's what keeps me alive. If I wasn't completely overwhelmed with my task, I would slip and let loose an inferno that could destroy the whole island."

"Oh," Sara nodded, and went back to walking. Ignis's project was so important, so dangerous. "You mean the volcano would erupt and take out the jungle, right?"

"No." Ignis shook her head. That was all Sara needed to hear. She realised that keeping back the eruption wasn't

Ignis's main task. She had to restore the jungle and gather new supplies. The volcano had actually been mostly dormant since the first eruption had consumed the jungle's southern point. It was their own fire that Ignis was struggling to keep in line. If they slipped for even a moment, they knew that they would let everything burn. Sara wondered if that was why they spoke so little - if it took all of their concentration to keep their powers under control, it was no wonder they hardly spoke. Sara could see it in

Ignis's eyes. Ms Thorpe had given them the jungle as a place to isolate themself when they needed it, to work on their project, but also to master their powers. They owed a lot to Ms Thorpe and her guardians - they owed a lot to the island. That was why they continued to work here, even though the volcano wasn't really an issue any more. Ignis might not have said more than a word, but all of a sudden, Sara understood so much more about them.

"Well, this is my stop," Sara noticed that they had reached the edge of the jungle, with the whole of Amity stretching out before them. "Good luck in there. I know you can do it,"

"Thanks," the response was off-hand enough, but Sara was pleased to know that Ignis had enjoyed their little walk.

"Until next time," Sara waved as she turned to leave, but found that Ignis had already disappeared back into the jungle. She hoped that in the time they all worked on the island, Ignis would master their inner fire and come out of their shell a little. Though they hadn't spoken much, Sara had enjoyed their company, and hoped to see them again some time.

Project Calypso was a big one, but one that Ignis had to work out on their own. There's nothing for me here, Sara thought, traipsing across Amity to find somebody else to help.

CREDITS

Daniel Stocks ©
Streetlights at Midnight, Poison
Memories, Breathing Colours,
Reckless. Overthinking, Empty
People, Rain in Summer, Fugitive

Rowan Costen ©
The Island Initiative, Eivor the
Undying, Legend of the Lotus, Eye of
the Storm

Aliyah White ©
Dilated Pupils, Patient 65, Mirror

Printed in Great Britain
by Amazon